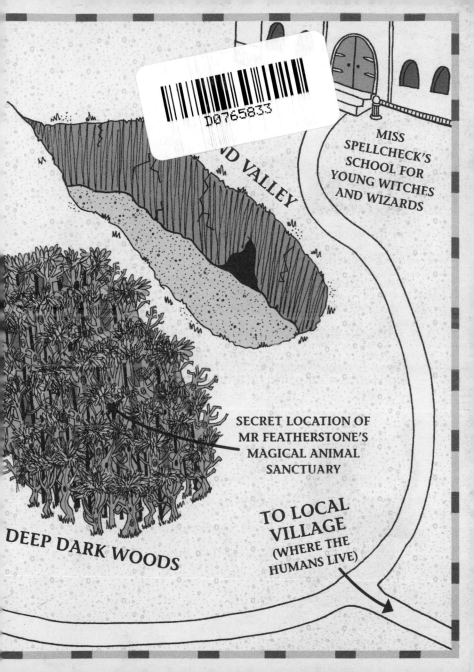

Meet the stars of
Mrs Mothwick's Magic Academy!

Sparky

Sparky is a fluffy, bouncy puppy
with brown and white splodges.
He is adventurous, playful and
very brave, and loves his wizard, Carl.
Mrs Mothwick's Magic Academy has
never allowed puppies in before, but
Sparky is trying hard to prove that he
can learn magic and be a good dog.

Sox

Sox is Sparky's best friend.
She is a sensible kitten with jet-
black fur and white paws. She
loves Sparky and does her best
to keep him out of mischief.

Trixie

Trixie is a sleek black cat. She's very good at magic but is a bit of a bully. She doesn't like dogs, so Sparky had better watch out!

Mrs Mothwick

Mrs Mothwick is head of the Magic Academy. She has a thin, warty face and wears a tall black

hat. Her familiar – her special animal friend with whom she has a magical bond – is a gruff vulture called Mr Carrion. She is proud of her Magic Academy, but she worries that her son, Carl, isn't ready to be a wizard.

Carl Mothwick

Carl is a bit clumsy and scruffy.
His shoelaces always seem to be
untied, and he smells of mud
and chewing gum. Even
though he tries really hard,
poor Carl just isn't very good at magic. He never
knows where his wand is, and even when he does
find it, he can't make it work the way the other
trainees can. Carl is desperate to prove to everyone,
including his mum, that he is a proper wizard.

Mrs Cackleback

Mrs Cackleback is the only
witch ever to own a
terrifying griffin as
her familiar, but
the less said about
her and her wicked
ways, the better . . .

Sparky's

School Trip

RUBY NASH

Illustrated by Clare Elsom

RED FOX

SPARKY'S SCHOOL TRIP
A RED FOX BOOK 978 1 782 95300 5

First published in Great Britain by Red Fox,
an imprint of Random House Children's Publishers UK
A Penguin Random House Company

Penguin
Random House
UK

This edition published 2015

1 3 5 7 9 10 8 6 4 2

Series created by Working Partners Limited
Copyright © Working Partners Limited, 2015
Cover and interior illustrations copyright © Clare Elsom, 2015
With special thanks to Pip Jones

Penguin Random House is committed to a sustainable future for
our business, our readers and our planet. This book is made from
Forest Stewardship Council® certified paper.

MIX
Paper from
responsible sources
FSC® C018179

Set in ITC Stone Informal

Red Fox Books are published by Random House Children's Publishers UK,
61–63 Uxbridge Road, London W5 5SA

www.randomhousechildrens.co.uk
www.totallyrandombooks.co.uk
www.randomhouse.co.uk

Addresses for companies within The Random House Group Limited can be
found at: www.randomhouse.co.uk/offices.htm

THE RANDOM HOUSE GROUP Limited Reg. No. 954009

A CIP catalogue record for this book is available from the British Library.

Printed and bound in Great Britain by CPI Group (UK) Ltd, Croydon CR0 4YY

For my lovely agent and friend,
Julia Churchill,
with thanks for everything x

Turn to page 200 for lots of
magical activities!

1

In the Courtyard of Mrs Mothwick's
Magic Academy, Sparky the puppy
was wagging his fluffy brown and
white tail.

"Our first ever school trip!"
he said to his best friend, Sox.

"I wonder where we're going."

"I can't wait to find out!" said Sox. The black kitten was bouncing up and down on her little white paws.

The Courtyard was filled with lots of excited animals. Bats, rats, mice, cats, pigs, squirrels, owls and frogs were all squeaking, chirping, mewing and croaking noisily. Gill,

a bright orange goldfish, blew a
happy bubble, which floated out of
his bowl and popped. They were all
familiars – magical animals who
helped witches and wizards – and
they were at the Academy to learn
how to do magic together.

*And now I can do a tiny bit of
magic too!* thought Sparky.

Unlike the other familiars, Sparky had arrived at the Academy by mistake. He wasn't magical at all, and no one had ever heard of a dog familiar before. But he'd tried very hard and had finally learned how to say a few words to his wizard, Carl. All familiars could talk to each other, and to Mrs Mothwick, but they had to make a special effort to be understood by other witches and wizards. And

Sparky had done it! As he thought about it, his tail wagged so hard that his bottom wagged a bit too.

"Look!" said Sox. "Here comes Mrs Mothwick!"

All the familiars went quiet as Mrs Mothwick, the headmistress, came marching towards them. Her black boots went **thud! thud!** and her long purple skirt *swished* around her ankles. A clipboard was tucked under her arm.

"**Good morning!**" she bellowed. "Now, before we go on our trip, we need to make sure everyone is here. Carl is going to take the register today, while I get the broom-bus ready to go. Hurry up, Carl!"

Sparky yipped with delight as he saw Carl running across the Courtyard, his shoelaces flapping. His hair was sticking up and his cheeks were pink. "Sorry I'm late, Mum!" he said as Mrs Mothwick

handed him the clipboard. "Come on, Sparky, you can help me."

As Carl scooped him up with his free hand, Sparky got a good view of the school motto carved into the wall in swirly writing:

Hand, fur and feather magic friends for ever.

That means Carl and I will never be separated, he thought. Sparky licked Carl's nose as he began reading out the names on the clipboard.

"Artie?" said Carl.

"Eee! Here!" squeaked a big brown rat. Sparky gasped when a glittery green tick magically appeared next to Artie's name.

Artie ☑
Bandit ☐
Derry ☐
Felix ☐
Sparky ☐
Trixie ☐
Toffee ☐

"Bandit?" Carl continued.

"Here!" replied Bandit, a bat who was hanging from the branch of a tree.

"Derry?"

"Yesssssss," hissed Derry, a yellow snake.

"Felix?"

A bright green frog croaked, "Here-rrrribbit!"

As each familiar answered, their name was magically ticked

off. "I know *you're* here, Sparky!" Carl laughed.

Sparky concentrated hard. **"Ruff! Hhh-ruff! Here!"** he barked, and a green tick appeared next to his name. *I did it! I'm learning to speak to Carl!* he thought happily.

"Trixie?" Carl continued.

There was no reply.

"Trixie?" he called again.

Sparky looked around the

Courtyard. Trixie wasn't there. He wriggled out of Carl's arms and jumped down next to Sox. "That's strange," he said. "It's not like Trixie to be late."

"No, it's not," Sox replied, rolling her eyes. "She's usually such a goody-four-paws."

Carl carried on. "Toffee . . . ?" he called. "Wilbur . . . ? And finally . . . Mr Carrion?"

Sparky was expecting to hear

the squawk of Mrs Mothwick's familiar, a grumpy old vulture. He frowned when he realized that Mr Carrion wasn't there either.

"Thank you, Carl," Mrs Mothwick said, taking the clipboard. "I don't know where Mr Carrion has got to, but no doubt he's attending to some important school business. Now, I'm sure you all want to know where we are going today, don't you?"

"Yes!" cried Sparky and all the familiars.

Mrs Mothwick smiled. "You'll have noticed that your witches and wizards aren't here today – except Carl, of course. That's because today is all about being a magical animal. We're going on a trip to Mr Featherstone's Magic Animal Sanctuary to meet some fantastical beasts!"

All the familiars gasped with delight.

"**Wow!**" yapped Sparky, his tail wagging. "I wonder what the Magic Animal Sanctuary will be like."

Sox's whiskers were twitching with excitement. "Maybe it'll be like the rescue centre, where we used to live," she replied. "I bet they don't have cages, though, because the animals could just use magic to open them!"

Mrs Mothwick clapped her

hands, and all the animals turned back to her. "That's not all," the witch continued. "The other *very* important purpose of this outing is to gather the magical ingredients we need to keep our school hidden from humans."

"Mrs Mothwick?" Sox raised one paw. "Why do we need to do that?"

"It is essential that we cast a **Hideaway Spell** to keep the Academy out of sight," Mrs Mothwick said gravely. "If humans ever discovered we were here, they would want us to do magic for them all the time. Things would never be the same again."

Sparky gulped.

"**Wowzers**, look!" Carl cried.

Sparky gazed up at the sky where he was pointing. High above, the air was shimmering and flickering strangely.

"Mum, is that the spell?" Carl asked.

Mrs Mothwick nodded. "The spell lasts one year, and it will wear off at sunset today," she told the class. "So we *must* be back in time. Today, nothing must go wrong. Now, let's—"

Just then Mrs Broth, the school cook, came rushing out of the entrance doors. She was holding a large basket.

"Here we are, my dears!" she said
breathlessly. "Packed lunches for
everyone! They have your names
on, and there is a little treat for
each of you too!"

As Carl took the basket from
her, Sparky stood on his back legs
to have a look. The basket was
full of neatly wrapped packages of
different sizes. Sparky knew which
one was his – he could smell the
dog biscuits inside.

Mmm! he thought, his tummy giving a grumbly rumble.

Suddenly a movement across the Courtyard caught Sparky's eye. Trixie was creeping through the school doors and scampering over to the group to stand quietly behind Mrs Broth.

Sparky was about to ask her why she was late, but then he noticed something red and sticky on one of her perfect black paws.

"Your paw needs a clean, Trixie,"
he said kindly.

She looked down and gasped in
surprise. Then she glared at Sparky.
"Well, at least I'm not a stinky
puppy like you!" she hissed.

Sparky's ears drooped. "I was just trying to help," he said. "I know how you like your fur to be shiny and beautiful."

"Ignore her, Sparky," Sox said. "You're not stinky. Trixie is just being mean, as usual."

Trixie turned her back on them and began hurriedly licking her paw clean.

A shadow passed over them as Mr Carrion swooped down. "Sorry

I'm late, Mrs Mothwick," said the old vulture, folding his huge black wings.

"Well, now you're here, we can go," Mrs Mothwick said briskly. "If you wouldn't mind, Mr Carrion, let's get the broom-bus into the air."

She led everyone towards a huge broomstick that was lying in the Courtyard. Mr Carrion hopped onto the front of the broom-bus, then Mrs Mothwick held her hands above the

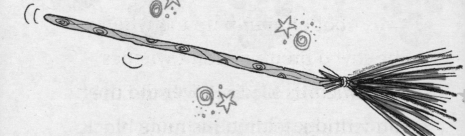

handle. There was a **puff** of glitter, and the broomstick rose smoothly into the air.

"Every witch needs a familiar's help to do magic," she reminded the class. "Even me. All aboard!"

The familiars hopped, jumped, flapped and slithered onto the school broom-bus. Finley the ferret did a backflip and landed perfectly

in the middle of the stick. Sparky
was about to jump up too when
he saw a group of adult witches
and wizards striding over the open
drawbridge into the school.

"Yip! Yip!" Sparky barked.
"Someone's coming!"

Mrs Mothwick gave a puzzled
frown as the visitors hurried
towards the broom-bus. Each of
them was holding an envelope.

I wonder why they're here, Sparky
thought.

"How nice to see you—" Mrs
Mothwick began.

But a man with fiery red hair interrupted her. "Is it true?" he demanded.

"Is *what* true?"

"Is it true that you're training an un-magic animal at this school?" snapped a woman with purple hair.

Sparky gave a **"Yip!"** of shock.

An un-magic animal . . . ? She means me!

Mrs Mothwick narrowed her eyes. "The school passed its inspection with flying colours just last week," she said. "This is the best school for familiars in the land."

"Nonsense!" the red-haired man cried. He thrust his envelope into Mrs Mothwick's hands. "It says so here – you've got an

un-magic animal at this school! It's
a scandal!"

Mrs Mothwick took out the letter
and read it quickly. "Who wrote
this?" she demanded.

"We don't know," the man
replied. "The letters were magicked
down our chimneys this morning."

"It doesn't matter who wrote
them," said the purple-haired
woman. "That's not the point! All
our children have familiars here.

I won't have my son George or his familiar mingling with an un-magic animal. I'm sending Gill to train at Lord Snootington's School for Familiars instead."

She scooped up Gill's goldfish bowl, making the water slosh over the side. Gill's eyes were wide. A bubble floated up to the surface and said "Hey!" as it popped.

Hey!

The other adults began gathering
up their children's familiars. A
woman with a pointy face picked

 up Artie and put
him in her bag.
Felix croaked
unhappily as he
was popped into a
man's top pocket.
Our friends!
thought Sparky miserably. *They're
taking them away because of me!*

"You're making a terrible
mistake!" Mrs Mothwick cried,
as more and more familiars were
plucked from the broom-bus.

"Lord Snootington's isn't nearly as
good as our academy!" Carl added
desperately.

But the adult witches and wizards
strode back across the Courtyard
and over the drawbridge, taking the
familiars with them. Now there were
only a few left on the broom-bus.

Mrs Mothwick's face went ghostly pale. "I bet *I* can guess who sent those letters," she said. "Mrs Cackleback! It's hard to believe that horrible witch and I were friends, before she turned to wicked ways."

Mrs Mothwick was still holding the letter and envelope. She scrumpled them up angrily, and Sparky gasped as he saw a seal on the back of the envelope: it was made of sticky red wax.

The red stuff on Trixie's paw! he thought. He knew that the snooty cat didn't like him being at the Academy. Sparky's tail drooped. *Trixie must have sent those horrible letters!*

2

Mr Carrion coughed and flapped his big wings. "Mrs Mothwick, shouldn't we be leaving for the Animal Sanctuary?" he said. "Mr Featherstone will be expecting us."

"Of course," said Mrs Mothwick,

stuffing the crumpled letter into
her skirt pocket. "I'm sure we can
sort this out later. But now we
have work to do. There are fewer
of us, but we still need to collect
the magical ingredients to keep
the school hidden. There's no time
to lose!"

The broom-bus was still floating
above the ground. The remaining
familiars held on tightly, while
Carl scooped up Sparky and

climbed onto the back. The animals
squeaked, chirped, yipped and
miaowed to say they were ready.
Mrs Mothwick sat on the front,
Mr Carrion just behind her,
holding Mrs Broth's basket in one
clawed foot.

"Hold on tight!" called Mrs
Mothwick, once they were all
aboard.

The broom-bus swooped up into
the air and over the wall of the

school. Far below, the huge trees of the **Deep Dark Wood** were swaying in the breeze. Sparky could smell leaves and grass – and something else. A tangy burning scent tickled his nostrils. Ahead, he saw wisps of white smoke curling up through the trees. He wanted to lean over the side of the broom-bus for a better look, but it was a long way down.

I don't want to tumble off! he

thought. *I know – Beady's got great eyesight.* He'd once hidden a marble under a stikwik bush, and Beady had spotted it from where she was perched on top of the school roof.

"Hey, Beady!" Sparky barked to the glossy crow who was perched next to Sox. "What's that down there?"

Beady blinked her shiny black eyes and peered down. "It's a campfire," she cawed. "I can see the

flames. There are children putting
up tents too!"

"**Wowzers!**" Sparky replied.

"Human Cub Scouts," Mrs
Mothwick called over her shoulder.
"They camp in the woods to learn
about nature and the outdoors."

"They're really close to our
school," Sparky said. "It's amazing
they can't see it."

"The **Hideaway Spell** is very
powerful," the headmistress replied,

"but unless we can find the magic ingredients, it'll fade away as the sun sets."

She began to steer the broom-bus down towards the wood.

Why are we going down? Sparky wondered. *I can't see anything but trees.*

He felt branches and leaves skimming his ears. He closed his eyes tightly, but opened them again when he heard the witch muttering a spell:

"Azz-a-bin! Azz-a-bash!
Lend magic light!
Bring Magic Sanctuary
Into our sight!"

The air around the trees sparkled
and shimmered for a moment, then
there was a **flash!** Six large
enclosures magically appeared.
In each one were beautiful
buildings, wooden huts and huge
magical plants with twirly leaves

43

and gigantic purple and yellow
flowers. Mrs Mothwick landed
the broom-bus next to a large
stone building with stained-glass
windows.

The door of the building flew
open, and a man with spiky
white hair and a bristly black
beard hurried out. He had three
clipboards and a bundle of maps
tucked under his arm.

"Welcome!" the man said,

shaking Mrs Mothwick's hand. "I have everything prepared."

"Thank you, Mr Featherstone," she replied.

The familiars and Carl hopped down from the broom-bus, and Sparky gazed around. The place

was full of strange scents. He sniffed
at a spiny orange plant in a pot;
it smelled like a cross between
tangerines and salty seashells.
When his nose touched the plant,
it wobbled and made a jingling
sound.

Sparky was about to show it to
Carl when another scent wafted
past – a horrible smell that he
knew very well.

He gave the air an extra good sniff,

just to be sure. It was definitely half lion, half eagle.

Oh no! he thought. *That's a griffin!*

Sparky's fur stood on end as he remembered the last time he'd smelled – and seen – a griffin. Horrible Mrs Cackleback had been riding on her griffin familiar when she tried to attack the Academy!

Whoosh! Whoosh! Whoosh!

There was a loud beating of
wings. Sparky turned to see the
huge creature swooping down
towards them. He gave a frightened
"Woof!" Sox dashed behind Mrs
Mothwick's legs, three white mice
called Harry, Larry and Sid squealed
and jumped into a plant pot,
and Beady flew high up into the
branches of a nearby tree, cawing
loudly as she went.

The griffin's talons raked deep

furrows in the ground as it landed beside them. Its enormous hooked beak glittered in the sunshine.

"Ah, hello, Tiffin!" Mr Featherstone said cheerily. He stroked the griffin's head.

Sparky yipped in astonishment. *I thought griffins were nasty!*

Mr Featherstone looked around at the frightened familiars. "Oh, you mustn't be afraid of Tiffin!" he told them. "Some griffins are wicked, but *this* griffin is a very good friend of ours."

"Hello," Tiffin said in a gentle voice. "It's lovely to meet you all."

Mr Featherstone handed out maps of the sanctuary, and the

familiars gathered around Mrs Mothwick.

"Listen!" she told them. "It's time for us to collect the three magical ingredients for the **Hideaway Spell**. We need—"

"I know!" Trixie piped up, striding out in front of Mrs Mothwick with her tail in the air. "We need a **golden egg**, a **phoenix feather** and a **shiny dragon's scale**."

"Yes, Trixie, very good," said Mrs Mothwick, a little impatiently. "So we shall split into three groups. Each group needs to meet one of the magical creatures and collect an ingredient from them. In Mr Carrion's group are Trixie, Beady, Samson and Spot."

Trixie sighed loudly. "Just my luck to get stuck in a group with a spider and a ladybird," she muttered. Samson the spider and

Spot the ladybird stepped out of Trixie's way as she pushed past them.

I'm glad I'm not in Trixie's group, thought Sparky, remembering the horrible letters. *She really doesn't like me!*

Harry, Larry, Sid and Bandit were in Mr Featherstone's group.

"That leaves Carl, Sparky, Sox, Pearl and Wilbur in my group," Mrs Mothwick said.

Pearl, a tiny pink piglet, oinked noisily. Wilbur, a fat brown toad, blinked his big yellow eyes twice.

The three groups set off in different directions. "This way," Mrs Mothwick called to her group, her purple skirt swishing as she set off down a path.

"Which animal are we meeting, Mum?" asked Carl.

"Fenella Goosey," said Mrs Mothwick. "She's the goose that lays golden eggs."

Carl grinned with delight. "Golden eggs? Amazing!"

"Yip! Yip! Yip!" said Sparky, dancing on his back legs. He decided not to worry about Trixie for now. He'd already met a friendly griffin, and now he was about to meet a magic goose. He couldn't wait!

MRS MOTHWICK'S MAGIC ACADEMY

3

Sparky trotted along happily at
Carl's heels, while Sox pranced
in and out of the strange-looking
plants lining the path. Wilbur was
too hot in the sunshine, so he was
riding on Pearl's back.

"Here we are!" Mrs Mothwick
said as they turned a corner and
arrived at a coop that looked like a
small wooden house. On the roof
was an elegant carving of a goose,
wings outstretched as if it was about
to take flight. In front of the coop
was a large pond.

"Why don't you take a dip,
Wilbur?" Sparky whispered. "It'll
cool you down."

"Great idea!" Wilbur
hopped into the water
and sat on a lily pad.

Mrs Mothwick
knocked on Fenella Goosey's door.
"Hello, Fenella!" she called politely.
"It's me, Mrs Mothwick."

Sparky listened hard, but there
was no reply.

"Fenella comes from a very long line of golden egg layers," Mrs Mothwick told them in hushed tones. "I do believe she is the one hundred and twelfth generation."

She knocked on the door again, a little louder this time. But there was still no answer.

"How strange," she said, frowning. "Fenella's such a polite bird. It's not like her to keep visitors waiting."

The witch hesitated for a moment, then gently pushed the door open and ducked inside. Sparky and the others followed.

Inside, the coop was cosy and warm. In the middle was a big nest of yellow straw lined with downy white feathers – but no golden egg.

"Fenella?" Mrs Mothwick called.
"Where are you?"

I bet I can sniff her out! Sparky
thought. He stuck his nose in the air.

Snuffling this way and that, he
caught a strong whiff of bird. He
followed the scent to a steep ramp
at the back of the coop, and began
to climb it. He was nearly at the top,
and the smell was getting stronger,
when suddenly there was a very loud
"HONK!"

"**Yip!**" Sparky jumped with surprise and slid all the way back down the ramp, knocking Sox over at the bottom.

"There you are, Fenella!" Mrs
Mothwick smiled.

Fenella was on a high platform
by the ceiling. She slowly stuck out
her long white neck, opened her
golden beak and gave a slow, sad

"Hoo-ooonk."

"We've come for a golden egg,"
Mrs Mothwick explained, "like we
did last year. You've usually laid one
by this time of day. Is everything all
right?"

Fenella slowly shook her head.
"No egg," she sighed. "I can't lay an
egg now. You'll have to come back
later."

Mrs Mothwick took a silver pocket
watch from the folds of her cloak
and bit her lip.

She's worried that we won't get the ingredients in time! Sparky thought.

He walked a little way up the ramp. "Are you upset about something, Fenella?" he asked.

"It was so terrible!" she cried. "I don't want to talk about it."

"It might make you feel better if you tell us," Sox suggested.

"Perhaps we can help," croaked Wilbur.

The goose gave another long

sigh. "It happened this morning," she began sorrowfully. "I was in my pond, taking my morning bath, when a horrible woman flew past and . . . she stuck her tongue out at me! Her tongue! Why would anyone be so mean and so . . . so *rude*!"

Sox snorted. "Is that all?" she giggled.

Sparky frowned at his friend. "You say this woman *flew* past?"

he asked Fenella. "What did she look like?"

She shook her head. "I'd rather not talk about her, if you don't mind."

Mrs Mothwick's foot was tapping on the floor impatiently. *How are we going to get an egg?* Sparky wondered. *Maybe Fenella would lay one if we could cheer her up?* He pawed at Carl's shoe with a **"Ruff!"**

Carl raised his eyebrows, looking puzzled, so Sparky tried again. **"Ruff! Truff! Trrr-icks!"**

"Good idea, Sparky!" Carl cried. "Fenella, Sparky's tricks always make me laugh. Maybe they'll help you forget about the mean woman. Ready, Sparky?"

"Yip!"

Mrs Mothwick, Sox, Pearl and Wilbur all stepped out of the way to give Carl and Sparky some space in the middle of the coop.

"Play dead!" said Carl.

Sparky lay perfectly still on the floor, his tongue lolling out of his mouth. Fenella

climbed off her ledge and waddled down the ramp, smiling. She sat in her nest to watch.

"On your feet!" said Carl. "And up!"

Sparky sprang up and lifted his front paws, so he was standing upright.

"Backwards twirl!"

Sparky skipped backwards in a
circle, his fluffy ears flapping.
Fenella laughed loudly, then gave a
little wiggle of her tail and stood up.

A golden egg! It was as big as
a tennis ball and glinted in the
sunshine that was pouring through
the door.

"Wonderful!" cried Mrs Mothwick,
picking it up carefully. "It's beautiful,
Fenella. Thank you."

"Thank you for cheering me up,"

said the goose. "I do feel much better."

Mrs Mothwick tucked the golden egg into her skirt pocket. "I wonder how the other groups are getting on," she said. "Carl, will you find Mr Carrion's group and check? They're at the phoenix enclosure."

"OK, Mum," Carl agreed.

"Can I go too, Mrs Mothwick?" Sparky asked, bouncing on his back legs.

"Me too?" Sox mewed.

"Yes, you may," Mrs Mothwick replied. She glanced at her watch again. "But hurry. There's no time to lose!"

MRS MOTHWICK'S MAGIC ACADEMY

4

Carl scratched his head and looked
again at the map he was holding.

"The phoenix enclosure must be
this way," he said, striding off along
a gravel path. Sparky and Sox
hurried after him.

"I can't wait to see what a phoenix looks like!" said Sparky.

"Me too!" Sox agreed.

Carl pointed towards a large open area encircled by fancy metal railings. "There it is! But look . . ."

Sparky followed Carl's gaze. Hovering right over the phoenix enclosure was a big dark cloud; rain was pouring down from it.

"Why is it raining inside the enclosure but nowhere else?"

Sparky wondered.

Sox shook her head. "I don't know. The rest of the sky is blue!"

Sparky bounded over to the railings and stuck his nose through. **Splat!** He shivered as a fat raindrop landed on his muzzle.

Inside, all he could see were big logs and piles of coal. *Where's Mr Carrion and his group?* he wondered.

"Here's the entrance," Carl called, pushing open a creaky gate.

Sox's whiskers twitched. "I'm not going in there," she said. "I'll get soaked!"

"Wait!" Sparky said. "Look! The rain's stopping."

He watched open-mouthed as the last raindrop fell. Then the dark cloud floated silently away.

"What weird weather," muttered Carl as they all went into the enclosure.

Trixie was crawling out from

under a log pile. She shook water
off her glossy black coat. "Ugh!" she
shrieked. "I'm wet through!"

Mr Carrion flapped out of the
logs too, followed by Samson, Spot
and Beady. The crow shivered
and shook some raindrops off her
feathers.

"Hello, Mr Carrion," said Sparky. "Why was it raining in here but not out there?"

Mr Carrion flapped his damp wings. "That had the hallmarks of a Bad Spell," he grumbled. "But I didn't see anyone. I don't know where it came from."

Carl told Mr Carrion and the others about Fenella. "Do you think the same woman who upset her made the rain cloud?"

Mr Carrion looked thoughtful. "It's very likely," he said. "We have to find Elfric the phoenix – we need one of his magical feathers for the **Hideaway Spell** – but that rain put his fire out. Without fire, phoenixes disappear."

Everyone gasped. Even Trixie's tail drooped.

"Poor Elfric," Sparky said. "We need to help him. Let's make another fire – it might bring him back!"

"It won't work," Mr Carrion
said gruffly. "Phoenixes don't like
ordinary fire. They need magical
fire." He peered down his hooked
beak at Sparky. "And like all things
magical, magical fires must be

made by a witch or wizard and
their familiar *together*. Sparky is
un-magic, so you two will not be
able to help."

Trixie sniggered. She gave Sparky
a cool stare, then licked her front
paw.

Still cleaning her paws! Sparky
thought crossly. *I bet she's thinking
about those horrid letters she sent,
telling everyone about me.* He gave
her a quiet growl.

"Mrs Mothwick and I will need to cast the spell together," Mr Carrion went on. "Beady, fly to Fenella Goosey's coop and fetch her. Hurry!"

Beady took off. Sparky watched her soar over the railings, wishing there was something he could do to help.

"There *is* something we can do," Carl said, as if he had read Sparky's mind. "Mum will need a nice dry stick to make a fire."

Sparky bounced up and down, wagging his tail. *I can find a stick – I'm good at that!*

Ignoring Mr Carrion's frown, he dashed out of the wet enclosure and put his nose to the ground. He scampered left and then right, ignoring the scents of beetles, birds and blackberry bushes, until he found himself under a huge oak tree.

Lying there was a long straight stick.

Perfect! Sparky picked it up in his mouth and carried it proudly back to the enclosure.

"Good dog!" Carl said, stroking Sparky's head. "See, Sparky isn't very magical, but he's really helpful!"

Sparky dropped the stick at the vulture's clawed feet. To his surprise, instead of saying thank you, Mr Carrion scowled at him.

Before long, Beady was swooping back over the railings, and a few moments later, Mrs Mothwick came hurrying through the gate.

"Sparky found a dry stick," Carl told his mum proudly.

"Thank you, Sparky," she said, picking it up. Mr Carrion flew onto her shoulder, then she muttered a spell:

"Fizzle-da-fazzle

Fizz-zip-dazap-zire!

Dizzle and dazzle

Come, magical fire!

As she spoke, the witch swirled the air with the stick. Mr Carrion opened his huge black wings and flapped them twice. Then, with a puff of green glitter, the end of the stick burst into purple flames.

"Wowzers!" Carl said.

Sparky huddled close to his legs as Mrs Mothwick lowered the flaming stick towards the ground.

Whoosh!

Purple, red, blue and green flames made a circle of fire in the middle of the enclosure.

"It's magical fire, so it's
completely safe," Mrs Mothwick
said.

Sparky went a little closer.
The colourful flames swirled and
danced, and in the middle of them
he saw something else moving too.

"Yip!" he said. "Look!"

"It's Elfric," said Mrs Mothwick,
smiling. "The fire is making him
appear again!"

Sparky watched, amazed, as the

shape in the flames grew larger.
Then a huge eagle-like bird rose
gracefully out of the fire.

"**Wowzers!**" cried Carl, his
eyes wide.

"**Double wowzers!**"
Sparky gasped.

Elfric's vast wings glowed red
and orange against the blue sky.
His long tail feathers shimmered
like flames.

Sox mewed in astonishment.
"Is he actually *made of fire*?" she
whispered.

Elfric landed neatly next to Mrs

Mothwick. He was as tall as she
was. "How are you, my old friend?"
he said with a bow.

"Very well, thank you," she
replied. "It's lovely to see you."

"I can't believe it's already time
for your **Hideaway Spell** again,"
the phoenix said. "Thank you for
helping me – I don't know why
it suddenly started raining! But,
anyway, here you go." He fanned
out his tail of glimmering feathers,
plucked the longest one with his
golden beak, and dropped it into
Carl's hand.

Carl stared at it.

"**Triple wowzers!**

It's not even hot. Thanks, Elfric!"

The phoenix bowed at him politely.

Mrs Mothwick looked at her watch, and then at the sky. The sun was getting lower.

"Carl," she said, "I think you'd better go and check that Mr Featherstone's group isn't having trouble getting the shiny dragon's scale. We've already had problems with two magical ingredients, and

we don't have any time to lose – the
Hideaway Spell will wear off soon."

"Of course, Mum," Carl agreed.
"Come on, Sparky, come on, Sox!"
The three friends bounded out of
the enclosure to find the Dragon's
Cave.

First Fenella couldn't lay an egg,
Sparky thought as they ran, *then the
rain made Elfric disappear. I wonder
what's going to happen next?*

MRS MOTHWICK'S MAGIC ACADEMY

5

As they hurried towards a huge dark cave surrounded by blackened rocks, Sparky got a sudden whiff of something strange. It smelled a bit like a lizard, but also like a bonfire. *So that's what a dragon smells like,*

he thought, his nose prickling. Sox's ears were pinned back with worry.

"Don't be scared!" Carl said to them. "All the creatures we've met so far have been really friendly. I'm sure the dragon will be too."

RO-AAAR!

A deafening noise echoed from the mouth of the cave.

"Yiiiip!" yelped Sparky.

"Miiaoow!" squealed Sox.

"Argghh!" yelled Carl.

Mr Featherstone bolted out of the cave. The ends of his beard were singed. "Get back!" he called to them. "He's in a terrible mood."

Harry, Larry and Sid rushed from the cave, and Bandit flapped behind them. He landed upside down on a branch, quivering.

Thud. Thud. **THUD.**

"The dragon's coming!" yelped
Sparky.

A massive head poked out of
the cave, red eyes glowing, smoke
hissing and billowing from its
flaring nostrils. The dragon was the
biggest creature Sparky had ever
seen – and he looked very angry.

THUDDD!

The dragon took a step towards
Carl and let out a deep, rumbly roar.

Carl's mouth dropped open. His eyes were wide.

I have to help! Sparky thought.

"Yip-yip-yip-yip-yip-yip!"

he cried, dashing between Carl and the terrifying creature. "You leave

Carl alone!" he growled as loudly as he could.

The dragon glared at Sparky, who trembled as he felt the heat of the creature's breath.

"Stop that noisy yapping!" the dragon bellowed. "Leave me alone! Why have all you little creatures come here to wake me up? All I want to do is sleep."

"We're v-v-very sorry, Santiago," Mr Featherstone stammered. "We

didn't mean to disturb you, but it's time for Mrs Mothwick's Magic Academy to do their **Hideaway Spell** again. They've come to ask you for one of your shiny scales."

Santiago huffed loudly. A flame flicked from his nose, followed by another huge cloud of smoke. "I've already been woken up by another visitor today," he said grumpily. "And as for a shiny scale, you won't get one of those from *me* today!" He

came all the way
out of the cave.
"Oh!" Sparky exclaimed.
"What happened to you?" Surely
dragons were supposed to be green,
but this one was brown all over,
from the end of his nose to the very
tip of his forked tail.

"Is that . . . mud?" Carl asked.

"Yes, it's mud, and it's all over me!" Santiago cried. "I can't get it off. I've tried to lick myself clean, but my hot breath just bakes the mud on even harder. I tried for ages and it's made me very tired, so if you don't mind . . ." He turned to go back into his cave.

Oh no! thought Sparky. *We need a scale!* "Wait!" he called. "How did you get yourself so muddy?"

"I didn't get *myself* muddy!" the dragon replied. "Someone made me muddy while I was asleep. I woke up and I looked like this."

Hmm, thought Sparky. *Could it have been the same person who upset Fenella and made it rain on Elfric?*

Carl sighed. "We really need a **shiny dragon's scale**," he said, "or Mum can't cast the spell to hide the school."

"Sorry," said Santiago, "but look

at me. I can't help you."

"There must be something we can do," said Sox.

What do I do when I'm muddy? thought Sparky. *I know!* He looked at Carl and concentrated as hard as he could.

"Bath!" he barked.

"Yes!" Carl cried. "Great
idea, Sparky! Santiago needs a
good bath. But, er, do you have
a bath that's big enough, Mr
Featherstone?"

Mr Featherstone's eyes shone.
"Not exactly," he replied. "But this
might be even better . . ." He took
a map of the sanctuary out of his
pocket and pointed to a large round
object in the middle.

"*Lake Lazuli*," Carl read, leaning

over to see. "Perfect! Santiago, we'll
have you clean and shiny in no
time!"

Mr Featherstone led the way
through the trees towards Lake
Lazuli. Sparky gazed up at
Santiago, who was walking next
to him. Every step the dragon took

made the ground shake. Sparky
was careful not to get too close to
his huge feet.

After a few minutes they came
to a large lake, its bright blue water
glinting in the sunlight.

"In you get, then," Mr
Featherstone said to Santiago.

The dragon frowned, and gave
the water a sniff.

Sparky waded in up to his
tummy and splashed the water
with his tail. **"Wowzers!"**
he yelled. "The water's lovely,
Santiago!"

The dragon puffed a little ring
of smoke from his nose, and then
slowly dipped one of his clawed feet
in. Some mud floated off and he
grinned. Then, with an enormous

splash!

he jumped right into the middle of
the lake. He flapped his huge wings,
spraying water over everyone.

Carl chuckled.
Sox spluttered
a little and
shook the water
off her fur.

"Santiago," Sparky giggled, "it
looks like you're having fun, but
to get you properly clean, we'll
have to give you a scrub."

Carl waded into the lake and
climbed onto the dragon's back.
He rolled his jumper into a ball and

started washing Santiago's wings.

Mr Featherstone removed
his jacket, and began cleaning
Santiago's tail. The dragon stretched
his long neck over to where Sox
and the mice were standing on
the shore, so they could clean his
face with their paws. Bandit flew
high above, showing Sparky where
the muddy bits were, and Sparky
jumped around to rinse the mud
away with great big splashes.

Soon Santiago's scales were
emerald green, glimmering like
jewels.

"Oh, thank you!" The dragon
smiled as he stretched out his
massive wings. "I feel so much
better. And now I can help you!"

Using a big shiny claw, he
scratched under his chin. A scale
as long as Sparky's tail fell to the
ground. Sparky picked it up gently
between his teeth.

"Now we've got everything we need to do the spell!" Carl grinned.

"**Yip!**" Sparky looked at the sun, which was already sinking in the sky. *And maybe just in time*, he thought.

MRS MOTHWICK'S MAGIC ACADEMY

6

"I thought I heard you!" Mrs
Mothwick called as she hurried
through the trees towards them.
"Do you have the scale?"

Sparky trotted forward and
proudly presented the **shiny**

dragon's scale, his tail wagging.

"We had to give him a bath first," said Carl as the witch took the scale from Sparky's mouth. "It was Sparky's idea."

"A bath?" Mrs Mothwick looked puzzled.

Carl nodded. "Someone tried to ruin Santiago's scales by making him all muddy."

Mrs Mothwick looked shocked.

But before
she could say
anything, there was
a hoarse squawk from above and
Mr Carrion landed beside them.
"Ah, I see you've got the third
ingredient," he said.

"We do. But there's something
very odd going on here," Mrs

Mothwick replied. "First a lady upset Fenella, then someone put out Elfric's fire, and now I hear that Santiago was splattered with mud. I think someone wants to stop us from gathering the magic ingredients we need."

Who could that be? wondered Sparky. He glanced up at Carl, who was biting his lip, looking uneasy. The puppy's fur prickled with worry.

"I know how to find out," said

Mrs Mothwick. "I'll use the Tell-tale Spell. It can be performed on Bad Deeds to show who's behind them. Please stand back, everyone – some lumps of mud from Santiago are still in the lake, and I'll need them for the spell."

Carl picked up Sparky and Sox, and they all stood next to the dragon. Mr Carrion hunched next to Mrs Mothwick so that her magic would work. The witch chanted:

"Ban-za-dang! Fing-la-fang!
Gan-wizz-da-tweel!
Who's done this Bad Deed?
Good magic, reveal!"

As she spoke, she waved her
wand over the muddy water. A
single twirl of black smoke snaked
out of the lake and into the air,
forming a small cloud. Suddenly
Sparky saw a face appearing in

the smoke. Dark
scraggly hair,
plump cheeks
– and a huge
brown mole
on the chin.

He yelped
in horror.
"It's Mrs
Cackleback!"
"Oh no!"
cried Carl.

"I should have known," Mrs Mothwick muttered, frowning. "First Mrs Cackleback sent those horrible letters, and now she's been trying to stop us from collecting the three magical ingredients."

"What if she's still here, Mum?" Carl asked.

Sparky shuddered, and licked the boy's face. The last time they'd seen Mrs Cackleback, she'd tried to steal the good witches' powers. Sparky

remembered the horrible sound of
her cackle as she swooped past on
her griffin, trying to catch Carl.

"The most important thing is
to get back to the school now,"
Mrs Mothwick replied, checking
her watch once more. "We must
do the **Hideaway Spell** before Mrs
Cackleback tries anything else.
Come on, the others will be
waiting for us at the gate.
Hurry!"

The witch ran off towards the trees, and they all dashed after her.

"Bye, Santiago!" Sparky called as he scampered along. "Bye, Mr Featherstone!"

The group ducked through archways of thorny bushes and followed the stony paths until they reached the gate. The other familiars chirruped and chattered when they saw Mrs Mothwick coming towards them. Sparky

and Sox skidded to a halt next to
Samson and Spot. The broom-bus
was lying on the ground.

"Quick, Mr Carrion," said Mrs
Mothwick. "Let's get everyone
aboard!"

As the giant broomstick started
to rise up off the ground, Sparky
smelled something odd. *What's that?*
He sniffed the air hard. The scent
was getting stronger, and it was
making the back of his neck feel all

prickly. *Half lion, half eagle!*

"**Ruff! Ruff! Ruff!**" Sparky barked in alarm and bounded over to Mr Carrion. "I can smell a griffin!"

"Well, of course you can," Mr Carrion said. "Tiffin's field is just over there." He lifted one black wing to point past some towering trees.

"I don't think it's Tiffin," Sparky said, shaking his head. "It smells different – it's more like—"

WHOOSH!

"Nee-hee-hee-hee!"

Sparky, Mrs Mothwick, Carl and
all the familiars gasped as a puff
of swirling black smoke appeared
in front of them. Standing in
the middle of it, her scraggly
black hair streaming out from
beneath her pointed hat, was Mrs
Cackleback.

"Still looking for your magical
ingredients?" she screeched.

"You!" Mrs Mothwick cried.

The wicked witch laughed loudly
and pointed a cruel finger at her.
"Yes, it was
me!" she yelled.
"It wasn't hard to upset
that wimpy goose. Or to put
out the phoenix's fire. As for that
dragon, I bet he's not quite
so proud of his scales now!
Nee-hee-hee-hee!"

Mrs Cackleback's awful cackle
was making the air quiver. Some of

the familiars were scrabbling
to hide under bushes, while
Samson and Spot nestled into
Sox's fluffy tail.

"How will you protect your
precious school now, Mrs
Mothwick?" Mrs Cackleback jeered.
"You can't cast the **Hideaway Spell**
without the three ingredients. Your
school will be discovered. It will be
closed down at once! I told you I
would have my revenge!"

"You're wrong!" Mrs Mothwick
boomed. "Thanks to Sparky here,
we *do* have the ingredients, all three
of them. Your plan didn't work!"

And she took the **shiny
dragon's scale**, the **phoenix
feather** and the **golden egg**
out of her pocket.

"Wha-aaaat?" Mrs Cackleback
shrieked. "Familiar, to me!"

***Whoosh! Whoosh!
Whoosh!***

Sparky looked up in horror as a huge griffin swooped down in front of them. Its eyes were wild and its beak looked as sharp as a blade.

The griffin began to nose-dive towards Mrs Mothwick. As it passed Mrs Cackleback, she jumped onto its back.

"Give those ingredients to me!"
she yelled.

Oh no! Sparky thought. *Mrs
Cackleback is going to ruin everything
after all!*

MRS MOTHWICK'S MAGIC ACADEMY

7

As the griffin dived down towards her, Mrs Mothwick turned to flee, but she tripped on a rock and tumbled over backwards.

Sparky watched, open-mouthed, as the precious magical ingredients

flew out of her hands, high into
the air.

Nooooo! he thought. He jumped
as high as he could, trying to catch
them in his jaws, but the griffin
zipped past and Mrs Cackleback
caught them in her hat.

"Give those back!" Carl shouted.

"Never!" The wicked witch
shrieked with laughter as the griffin
zigzagged away over the trees.

Mrs Mothwick jumped to her feet

and swiftly pulled out her wand.
She flicked it hard, and a golden
spark shot through the
air like lightning. But
the griffin
twisted to
one side and
the magic
narrowly
missed
its tail.

"Go after them, Mum!" Carl cried.

Mrs Mothwick shook her head sadly. "I'll never catch them, son. Maybe if I had my own broomstick here, I could, but the broom-bus is just too slow."

"How long before the **Hideaway Spell** wears off?" Mr Carrion asked gruffly.

"Only an hour." Mrs Mothwick gave a groan. "Those human Cub

Scouts will soon be able to see the school."

Sparky watched helplessly as the griffin's huge wings carried Mrs Cackleback off into the distance. *We've got to do something,* he thought. *Wait! Those huge wings . . .*

"We need *wings*!" Sparky shouted excitedly, wagging his tail.

Mr Carrion peered down at the puppy and tutted. "What on earth are you talking about?"

"We need *great big wings!*" Sparky
cried. "Sox, follow me – I've got a
plan!"

He turned and darted back along
the stony path.

Sox caught up with him. "Where
are we going?" she asked.

"To ask Santiago for help,"
Sparky panted as he ran. "The
broom-bus can't catch a griffin,
but maybe a dragon can!"

Sparky and Sox didn't stop running
until they reached Lake Lazuli.

Santiago was back in the water
again, breathing out hot air
through his nostrils and making the
water bubble.

"Santiago!" Sparky called.
"Santiago, help!"

The dragon swam quickly
towards the shore and climbed out.
"What is it?" he asked.

"That evil witch who got you
muddy," Sparky panted, "she's
stolen the three magical ingredients

and flown away on her griffin. We have to get them back – otherwise our school will be discovered and—"

"Climb aboard!" Santiago bellowed, lowering his snout to the ground. Sparky scrambled on carefully, aware of the heat from the dragon's nostrils. Sox followed, and they clambered over Santiago's head and slid down his long, scaly neck until they were sitting on his back.

"Hold on tight!" he shouted as he unfolded his massive wings. Taking long strides, he flapped once, twice, three times and

... *WHOOSH!*

"Wowzers!" Sparky yelled as they soared into the air.

Every beat of Santiago's wings made the puppy's ears flutter, and he found it difficult to catch his breath.

"I've never flown this fast before," he cried. "Not even on Mrs Mothwick's broomstick!"

"We're so high up!" Sox squealed, gazing at the Magic Animal Sanctuary far below. "Can

you see them, Santiago?"

The dragon turned sharp
right, making Sparky's tummy
somersault.

"There they are," he called.
"They're heading for **Wildwood
Thicket**."

With a deafening flap of his
sparkling green wings, Santiago
flew even faster. Sparky could see
Mrs Cackleback and her griffin now.
They were catching up with them!

The witch turned to look over
her shoulder, and scowled when she
saw Santiago, Sox and Sparky. "You
foolish do-gooders!" she cried.

The griffin swung to the left,
looped the loop, then zoomed
straight towards Santiago.

"He's going to get us!" Sox
wailed.

The dragon darted to the right,
but Mrs Cackleback's griffin
swooped after him. The rush of air

as they sped past made Sparky's paws slip on the dragon's scaly back.

"Yip! Yip! Yip!" he cried. "I can't hold on!"

Behind him, Sox reached out and grabbed his fluffy tail with her claws, dragging him back to safety.

"Are you safe?" Santiago asked.

"I'm OK now," Sparky panted.

"Then hold on tight." Beating down with his wings, the dragon sped after Mrs Cackleback and the griffin. They were still zooming towards **Wildwood Thicket**. The dragon inhaled deeply and roared so loudly that the air shook. Sparky felt the heat rising from his scaly back.

Then a gigantic tongue of fire

shot out of Santiago's mouth and streaked across the sky, showering the griffin and Mrs Cackleback with flaming sparks.

Grabbing her pointy hat, the witch flicked the sparks away. As she did so, the **golden egg**, the **shiny dragon's scale** and the **phoenix feather** tumbled out of the hat.

Mrs Cackleback shrieked with horror.

"The magical ingredients!"
Sparky cried. "Let's get them!"

Santiago dipped his long
neck and went into a nose-dive.

"**Oof!** Got it!" Sparky said
as he caught the heavy golden
egg in his front paws.

Next Santiago skimmed past
the falling shiny scale, and Sox
caught it in her teeth. The
beautiful phoenix feather
drifted slowly down.

Santiago gave a little puff and blew it towards Sparky, who grabbed it neatly with his jaws.

"**Nooooo!**" Mrs Cackleback shrieked. Shaking her fist, she lost her balance as the griffin flapped awkwardly towards the thicket. She managed to grab hold of its tail, but her feet caught in the treetops. **CRASH!** They flew

straight into the branches of a
Spindle Spike tree.

As Santiago flew over, Sparky
saw that Mrs Cackleback's cloak was
hooked over a spiny branch, leaving
her dangling, while the griffin's right
wing was stuck fast to a cluster of
spindly prickles.

"Serves you right!" Sox called.

Santiago blew a puff of hot
smoke in Mrs Cackleback's direction.
The witch groaned, and started

pulling Spindle Spikes out of her straggly hair.

"I can't thank you enough, Santiago," Mrs Mothwick said with delight as Sparky and Sox carefully placed the three magic ingredients at her feet.

"My pleasure," the dragon replied. "But now I'm very tired, so I think I'll go and take a nap. See you next year!" He gave a very

noisy, hot yawn, then flew off in the direction of his cave.

Mrs Mothwick knelt down and ruffled Sparky and Sox's ears. "Thank you both too," she said. "Now we can cast the **Hideaway Spell** before the sun goes down."

Sparky wagged his tail so hard it was a blur, and Sox's loud purrs made her fur quiver.

Mrs Mothwick and Mr Carrion raised the broom-bus, and all the

animals hopped or crawled aboard.
Carl quickly took the register once
again, and then handed each of the
familiars the treats that Mrs Broth
had packed for the journey home.

Sparky used his teeth to unwrap
the paper.

"Yum!" he said
when he saw four big
dog biscuits and
a scrumptious-
looking toffee

cupcake covered in sticky red icing
and a large white marshmallow.

"Hey!" said Sox. "Who's been
nibbling on my cupcake? Some of
the icing has gone!"

Sparky looked at his cupcake
closely. "Oh, yes. Mine
too."

In front of
Sparky, Trixie's
ears flattened
a little.

"Well, mine looks fine," she said loudly.

Sparky gasped.

Trixie's paws! he remembered. *So it was red icing she was cleaning off them this morning. It wasn't wax from the letters at all!*

Sparky was glad that Trixie hadn't sent the horrible letters, but he felt a nagging sense of worry in his tummy. In that case, who *had* sent them?

MRS MOTHWICK'S MAGIC ACADEMY

8

Over the Courtyard, the warm sun
was slowly edging its way down the
brilliant blue sky. The broom-bus
landed safely, and they all climbed
off.

"That was a *very* exciting day,"
said Carl.

As Mrs Mothwick hitched up her
purple skirt and climbed down, he
and Sparky saw something fall out
of her pocket.

Thinking it was one of the
ingredients, Sparky darted over
to pick it up. But it was one of the
horrible letters sent to the witches'
parents. He remembered Mrs
Mothwick crumpling it up and
putting it in her pocket before they
went on the trip.

Sox trotted over and sniffed the letter. Her ears were pricked, and Sparky knew that she was thinking hard.

"Mrs Mothwick," Sox said, holding the letter with one little white paw. "You know the Tell-tale Spell you did on the mud? If you do it on this letter, won't it tell you who wrote it?"

Mr Carrion flapped his wings. "What a ridiculous idea!" he

squawked, so loudly it made the familiars jump. "We have much more important work to do – casting the **Hideaway Spell** to protect the school!"

Mrs Mothwick glanced up at the sky. "The sun is setting," she said, "but it hasn't reached the tops of the trees yet, so we still have plenty of time to do the Tell-tale Spell! Good idea, Sox. Please hand me the letter."

Mr Carrion shook his feathers again. "Mrs Mothwick," he said, "I really don't think it matters who sent those letters—"

"Nonsense, Mr Carrion," she said. "I need to know if Mrs Cackleback wrote them – or someone else."

Mr Carrion began flapping his large black wings and hopping from one clawed foot to the other. But Mrs Mothwick ignored him and chanted the spell:

"Ban-za-dang! Fing-la-fang!
Gan-wizz-da-tweel!
Who's done this Bad Deed?
Good magic, reveal!"

There was
a *puff* of green
glitter in the air.
Black smoke
began to swirl
out of the letter
Mrs Mothwick
was holding.
It twisted and

twirled, making shapes in the air. Sparky watched, entranced. First he saw two hooded eyes ... then a bald, wrinkled head ... a sharp, hooked beak and hunched black wings ...

"No! That's Mr Carrion!" he barked. Everyone in the Courtyard gasped loudly. Carl's mouth dropped open.

173

The letter fell out of Mrs Mothwick's
hand. Her eyes were wide with shock.

All the events of the morning
whizzed through Sparky's head. The
angry parents said that the letters had
arrived that morning. *That's why Mr
Carrion was late, and didn't explain why,*
Sparky realized. *He was magicking the
letters down their chimneys!*

Mrs Mothwick had clearly put it all
together too. "How *could* you?" she
said quietly, her eyes glistening with

tears. "How could you betray our school like this?"

Mr Carrion puffed up his chest. "I did it to *protect* the school," he said. "Ordinary animals like Sparky cannot be trained to do magic. It's not right."

Sparky's ears drooped. He was already upset that Trixie wanted him sent away, but a *teacher*? He'd been trying so hard in all his lessons . . .

Mrs Mothwick fixed her icy blue eyes on Mr Carrion. "Whatever you think about Sparky being here," she said gravely, "you leave me no choice. You have broken the most important rule. The motto of this school is **Hand, fur and feather, magic friends for ever.** Total loyalty to your witch."

"Yes, but—" the vulture spluttered.

Mrs Mothwick interrupted him.

"Mr Carrion . . ." She paused for a moment. "You are no longer my familiar."

Sparky and Sox gasped. All the other familiars squeaked, chirped and squawked in surprise. Carl's mouth opened even wider.

Mr Carrion opened his beak
to speak, but then closed it again
without uttering a word. For a
moment he looked unhappily at
Mrs Mothwick. Then he turned,
opened his great black wings, and
flew high into the sky and off into
the sunset.

"Mum?" Carl whispered. He
touched Mrs Mothwick's arm.

The witch patted his hand. Her
eyes looked sad.

"Hey, what's that?" Sox asked, breaking the silence.

From just over the wall, Sparky heard voices singing and laughing.

"Oh, goodness," Mrs Mothwick cried. "The human Cub Scouts! They're getting closer. We really must cast the **Hideaway Spell**, but—" She suddenly looked pale.

"What's the matter?" Carl asked.

"Mr Carrion has gone," she replied, "and like all spells, the

Hideaway Spell must be cast by a witch and her familiar together."

Oh no! Sparky thought in horror.

But Carl looked determined. "*We'll* do the spell," he said. "Sparky and I will do it."

Us? Sparky thought. *Yes, us! We'll do it!*

Mrs Mothwick looked from

Sparky to Carl. "Oh dear," she said after a pause. "It's a very complicated spell . . . but yes, I think you're going to have to try. We don't have any choice!"

Sparky pricked up his ears, ready to do whatever was needed.

Trixie tutted. "Goodness knows what'll happen now. If *my* witch was here, we'd be safe, but—"

Ignoring her, Mrs Mothwick took the magic ingredients out of her

pockets. "First we'll need a cauldron," she said. Carl ran off to fetch one.

"Sparky," she went on, "you and Carl will need to start a magical fire to make the cauldron bubble, so you'll need to find a—"

"A stick!" Sparky yipped. He dashed across the drawbridge and sniffed out a long straight stick before returning to the group and dropping it next to the cauldron Carl had brought back.

"Here," Mrs Mothwick said, handing Carl the three magic ingredients. "Ready?"

"Ready as we'll ever be," he replied.

Carefully, Carl dropped the **golden egg**, the **phoenix feather** and

the **shiny dragon's scale** into the
cauldron.

"Now for the magical fire," Mrs
Mothwick said. "Do you remember the
spell I cast in Elfric's enclosure?"

"I think so," Carl said. He
picked up the stick and
held it in front of him.

"Yip!" Sparky
pressed up against
Carl's legs, and
concentrated

184

as hard as he could.

Carl waved the stick and began
to say the magic words:

"Fizzle-da-fazzle

Fizz-zip-dazap-zire!

Dizzle and dazzle

Come, magical fire!

Everyone in the Courtyard was
silent. *Come on!* Sparky thought to
himself. *Come, magical fire!*

Suddenly he felt tingly and hot,

as if his tummy was full of popping bubbles. He wagged his tail, and gave three loud yips.

Immediately there was a tiny *puff!* Sparkles of green glitter floated in the air and then – **flash!** The end of the stick burst into flames.

"Wowzers!" Carl cried. "We did it, Sparky! We did some magic!"

Sparky gasped, then grinned. **"Yip, yip yip!"** We did it!

"Well, I never!" Mrs Mothwick

exclaimed, clapping her hands with delight. "Well done!"

"Hooray for Sparky!" Sox cheered. Even Trixie seemed to have forgotten to be annoyed, and her

eyes were wide with surprise.

Carl held the burning stick to the bottom of the cauldron. It quickly began to bubble.

"Now for the **Hideaway Spell**," Mrs Mothwick said. "I'll help you with the words, but you and Sparky *must* be the ones to cast it."

Carl looked serious. Sparky took a deep breath.

Mrs Mothwick whispered the words to Carl, and he said the spell aloud:

"Wizz-abra-dash! Van-ishra-dash!

Bestow for one year!

Envelop with magic!

Make school disappear!"

Sparky concentrated on the spell. With every word that floated through his mind, his skin felt

warmer, his paws more tingly. His belly was all bubbly again, and his tail wagged so hard he thought it might fly away. He let out three noisy yips, just as he had done before.

Puff! Green glitter burst over the cauldron. Carl lifted Sparky up so that he could see inside, and he gasped at the sight of the ingredients whirling around. The feather and dragon's scale started

to melt. Then the egg started melting
too, and soon the cauldron was filled
with a shimmering liquid swirl of
red, gold and green.

The cauldron rumbled, then –

BOOM!

The liquid exploded with a flash
of light so bright that Sparky had to
cover his eyes with his paws.

Peeping out, he saw white sparks
zooming over everyone's heads and
shooting straight up in the air.
Above the high walls of the
school, the blue sky twinkled and
shimmered with dazzling stars.
Sparky glanced around and saw
that Mrs Mothwick, Carl and all the
familiars were gazing upwards, their

mouths wide open. He knew they were wondering the same thing as he was. *Has the spell worked?*

Slowly the stars faded. Then laughter rang out. Everyone turned at once, and saw a group of Cub Scouts walking along on the other side of the drawbridge. The boy at the front seemed to be looking directly at the school.

"Look!" he said, pointing. His friends turned to see what it was.

Had they discovered Mrs Mothwick's Magic Academy? Sparky held his breath . . .

"I told you!" the boy said. "A toadstool!" And he bent down to peer at a large red toadstool growing beside the drawbridge.

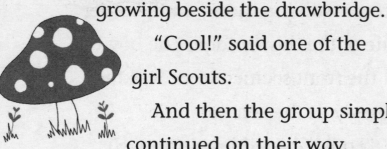

"Cool!" said one of the girl Scouts.

And then the group simply continued on their way. Sparky gave a yip of

amazement.
The Scouts
hadn't
seen the
huge school
building at all!
"It worked," he cried.
"Our magic *worked*!"

"You did it!" Mrs Mothwick
grinned. "Our school is safe!"

Carl hugged Sparky tightly,
and Mrs Mothwick threw her arms

around them both and hugged
them too. All the familiars cheered.
Sox was darting around in happy
circles, and even Trixie was smiling
– though she quickly covered her
mouth with her tail.

Mrs Mothwick gently took Sparky
from Carl. "Well, well," she said as
she smiled at him. "It's fascinating."

"What's fascinating?" he asked.

"It would seem that Mr Carrion
was wrong," the witch replied,

ruffling Sparky's ears. "He said
un-magic animals couldn't be
trained to do magic – but you,
Sparky, just *did magic*."

"So . . ." Sparky paused and
frowned a little. "Does that mean
I was magic all along, and I just
didn't know it?"

"I don't think so, Sparky," the
witch replied. "But I do think it
means that any animal *can* be
trained to do magic. Even a bouncy,

cheeky little puppy like you!"

Sparky licked Mrs Mothwick's nose happily and she handed him back to Carl.

Carl was grinning. "Now that Sparky can do magic, we don't have an un-magic animal at the school after all. We can tell all the parents that the other familiars can come back!"

"That's right," Mrs Mothwick said, and the other familiars cheered.

"Ruff! Ruffrr! Friends!" Sparky barked, patting Carl's tufty hair with his paws.

"That's right, boy!" Carl laughed. **"Hand, fur and feather, Magic friends for ever."**

For ever! Sparky smiled, so happy he thought he might burst. *For ever and ever!*

Read on for some magical games and activities!

Mr Carrion's Cunning Quiz

1) Which three magic ingredients does Mrs Mothwick need to find?

2) What is the name of the Magic Animal Sanctuary's friendly griffin?

3) Who owns the Magic Animal Sanctuary?

4) What animal is Beady?

5) What happened to Santiago when he was asleep?

6) Where does Santiago go to have his bath?

7) What colour are the cupcakes?

8) Who is responsible for posting the nasty letters?

Turn to the back of the book to see the answers!

Communication Code Breaker

Help Sparky and Carl communicate! Using the code below, can you work out what Sparky is saying?

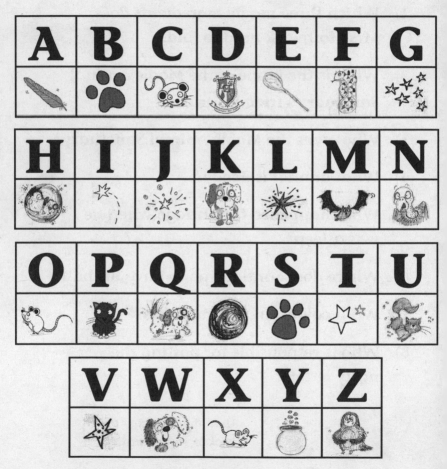

1)

   — — —

2)

   — — — — —

3)

   — — — —

4)

   — — — — — —

5)

   — — — — —

Turn to the back of the book to see the answers!

Egg Hunt

There are five golden eggs hidden in this picture. Can you find them all?

Spot the Difference

There are five differences between
these two pictures.
Can you find them all?

Turn to the back of the book to see the answers!

Witchy Wordsearch

Ten words are hidden in the wordsearch. Can you find them all?

Dragon

Broomstick

Cupcake

Egg

Feather

Goose

Scout

Carl

Sparky

Elfric

N	O	G	A	R	D	W	Q	Y	X
U	B	F	E	A	T	H	E	R	F
L	R	X	I	H	Q	L	G	G	E
I	O	U	K	E	W	F	X	L	K
X	O	S	P	A	R	K	Y	U	A
O	M	Q	F	E	K	U	Q	W	C
W	S	E	L	F	I	A	E	X	P
L	T	S	U	X	B	F	I	L	U
O	I	O	Q	T	P	I	R	L	C
X	C	O	F	W	T	A	U	I	W
Q	K	G	X	S	C	O	U	T	C

Turn to the back of the book to see the answers!

Mrs Mothwick's Maze

Find the shiny dragon's scale in the middle of
the maze, but avoid the muddy puddles –
and Mrs Cackleback!

start

Turn to the back of the book to see the answers!

Broomstick Ride

Help Mrs Mothwick and her class find their way
back to the Academy. Which route should they take?

Answers

Mr Carrion's Cunning Quiz:

1) A golden egg, a shiny dragon's scale and a phoenix feather
2) Tiffin
3) Mr Featherstone
4) A crow
5) He got covered in mud by Mrs Cackleback
6) Lake Lazuli
7) Red
8) Mr Carrion

Communication Code Breaker:

1) Egg
2) Scale
3) Bath
4) Trixie
5) Spell

Egg Hunt

Witchy Wordsearch

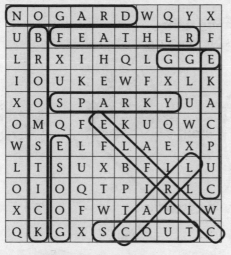

Mrs Mothwick's Maze:

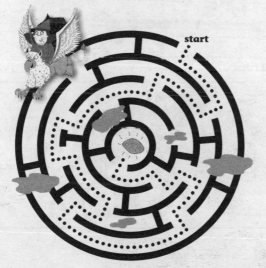

Broomstick Ride

Spot the Difference

Coming Soon!

Sparky's Magic Show

Don't miss Sparky's next adventure!